CHOOSE YOUR OWN ADVENTURE®

Kids Love Reading
Choose Your Own Adventure®!

"I like to follow the unicorn in the haunted house. I like to wonder what is going to happen with the unicorn and I."
Lilly Boyd, age 6

"This book is fun. It's fun to make choices and you might find a big fat bat."
Blaise Mackenzie, age 6

"I like how you can make up the story, but it also tells you a story."
Liam Stewart, age 6

"I give it at least...I would give it six stars, but there's only five, so I give it five stars."
Soren Bay-Hansen, age 7

"I liked when you went up the golden stairs!"
Libby Ringer, age 6

"I think this story is really wacky...I don't think I should tell you any more than that. It's a surprise."
Azailea Morales, age 8

Illustrated by: Keith Newton
Book and cover design by: Stacey Boyd

For information regarding permission, write to:

CHOOSECO

P.O. Box 46
Waitsfield, Vermont 05673
www.cyoa.com

A DRAGONLARK BOOK

Publisher's Cataloging-In-Publication Data
Names: Montgomery, R. A. | Newton, Keith (Illustrator at Chooseco LLC), illustrator.
Title: The haunted house / by R.A. Montgomery ; illustrated by: Keith Newton.
Other Titles: Choose your own adventure. Dragonlarks.
Description: [Revised edition]. | Waitsfield, Vermont : Chooseco, [2011] | Originally published:
Toronto : Bantam Skylark Book, ©1981. Choose your own adventure ; 2. | Summary: An adventure
story featuring a dog that disappears into an abandoned, possibly haunted, house. You make choices
throughout the story which will determine the outcome.
Identifiers: ISBN 1933390514 | ISBN 9781933390512
Subjects: LCSH: Haunted houses–Juvenile fiction. | Dogs–Juvenile fiction. | CYAC: Haunted houses–
Fiction. | Dogs–Fiction. | LCGFT: Action and adventure fiction. | Choose-your-own stories.
Classification: LCC PZ7.M7684 Hau 2011 | DDC [Fic]–dc23

Published simultaneously in the United States and Canada

Printed in China

19 18 17 16 15 14 13 12 11

CHOOSE YOUR OWN ADVENTURE®

THE HAUNTED HOUSE

BY R.A. MONTGOMERY

ILLUSTRATED BY KEITH NEWTON

A DRAGONLARK BOOK

To Shanny, Becca, Avery, and Lila

READ THIS FIRST!!!

WATCH OUT!
THIS BOOK IS DIFFERENT
from every book you've ever read.

Do not read this book from the first page through to the last page.

Instead, start on page 1 and read until you come to your first choice. Then turn to the page shown and see what happens.

When you come to the end of a story, you can go back and start again.
Every choice leads to a new adventure.

Good luck!

You and your dog Homer are walking home from school for lunch one day. Since he loves to play, you pick up a stick from the sidewalk and give it a big toss. Homer goes after it.

A white cat runs in front of him and— *zoom!*—Homer chases the cat. Homer chases her right into the yard of a big gray house.

Turn to the next page.

Wow! It looks as if nobody has lived here for years. The grass is uncut. The front door is half open. Most of the windows are broken, and there are shingles missing from the roof. It's definitely a scary-looking old house. Maybe it's haunted!

Homer is nowhere in sight. You call out for him.

"Homer! Hey, Homer! Come back, Homer."

NO ANSWER.

You have to find Homer. He's your friend. You enter the front yard through the old, rusty gate. You tiptoe around to the back of the house. You see a stone bench and an empty fish pond, but no Homer.

You sit down on the bench to think for a minute. Even though it's warm out, the stone bench makes you feel very cold. All of a sudden there is an icy gust of wind. You are freezing! You hear a voice coming from inside the house!

Turn to the next page.

"HOMER IS IN THE HOUSE."

The voice is deep and loud, and very, very scary. You want to find Homer, but that voice is so awful that you don't want to go near the house. What should you do?

If you run away, turn to page 7.

If you go into the house, turn to page 11.

It's creepy going down into the cellar.

A bat swoops low. Rats scurry about. A river runs through the cellar! There is a blue boat tied to a metal ring in the wall.

*If you get into the boat,
turn to page 23.*

*If you walk along the bank,
turn to page 37.*

You run faster than you've ever run before. Suddenly you fall down some stairs.

You are knocked out. You see stars. When you wake up, you are inside the house! It is very dark and dusty. You are terrified!

If you scream for help, turn to page 15.

*If you stay quiet and wait,
turn to page 17.*

You follow the mysterious unicorn outside. You can jump a mile high! You can even fly! You are having so much fun that you nearly forget about Homer!

If you continue on with the unicorn, turn to page 20.

If you want to find Homer, turn to page 21.

The crocodile crawls toward you and snaps again. It catches you by the shirt. The shirt rips. The crocodile grabs you by the sneaker. It pulls you into the water. Ughhh!

Turn to the next page.

It's funny, though—the crocodile's teeth are not sharp. They feel like rubber teeth. And the water is warm and comfortable.

Turn to page 64.

"After all," you say to yourself, "this is just an empty house. It's not really haunted." You decide to go in through the boarded-up back door.

Turn to the next page.

You pull a board aside and push the door open. *Creak!!* It is damp inside and smells like an old sneaker. You tiptoe into the dark room, holding your breath so you won't make any noises. From the darkness, a unicorn appears. It looks at you and disappears into the darkness.

If you try to follow the unicorn, turn to page 8.

If you're not sure what to do, turn to page 14.

This is scary! Maybe you should go home. But you can't leave Homer. You and he are pals. He is a great dog. Maybe the unicorn is a friend. Maybe it knows where Homer is.

Wham! A door slams somewhere in the back of the house. Cobwebs brush over your face. The same voice says, "Go down to the cellar."

If you obey the voice, turn to page 6.

If you decide to stay where you are, turn to page 16.

You hear the *thump, thump* of your own heart. You feel so scared and alone that you scream for help. A bat flies by. He is as big as you are! He says, "I'll help you. Just climb on my back."

It might be useful to have this bat as a friend.

If you fly with the bat, turn to page 26.

If you hide from the bat, turn to page 28.

You stay where you are. A trapdoor swings open. You climb down the rickety ladder and find yourself in a bright room. The room is filled with mirrors that make you look very, very tall or very, very fat or very, very skinny.

Turn to page 48.

Time doesn't seem to pass. The darkness gets darker. You are too terrified to breathe. You want to go home.

Then it happens. A furry thing touches your hand.

Ick! Yuck! Could it be Homer?

If you don't want to find out, turn to page 31.

If you want to find out, turn to page 45.

"Okay, Mr. Mouse, lead the way."

He grins at you. His nose twitches in a cheerful way like a rabbit's. The two of you push aside a blue curtain and go down a flight of stairs. The mouse shows you two keys. One is gold and the other is silver.

There are two doors in front of you. They are made of wood and have big locks. One lock is silver and the other is gold.

The mouse holds out the two keys and says, "Go ahead. You choose."

If you take the silver key, turn to page 50.

If you take the golden key, turn to page 69.

You follow the unicorn higher and higher. Soon it stops on a cloud. Sun shines right through it. It smiles at you. Then it walks up on a sunbeam.

You follow it. When you look back, the scary house is just a little gray dot.

Maybe it's time to turn around.

If you want to see where the sunbeam takes you, turn to page 33.

If you do turn back and leave the unicorn, turn to page 71.

Thump! You bump into a wall and fall onto the floor. Your journey with the unicorn ended quickly. You're back in the haunted house again.

Turn to the next page.

You hear a noise. You are frightened. A door opens. A boy your own age comes out of a room. It's your best friend Anson! On one hand he has a baseball glove and in the other hand a baseball.

Turn to page 25.

Boats are fun. When you get into the blue boat, the oars lift up just as if they were alive. They begin to row themselves! The boat takes you to the other side of the river.

A light flashes, then a voice says, "Either get out here or go on to the next stop. Have the correct fare ready, please."

If you get out, turn to page 43.

If you stay in the boat, turn to page 47.

You made a big mistake. The candy turns you into a furry turtle.

The End

You tell him everything that has happened. Anson smiles and says, "Haunted houses sure are fun. I know some great places in this house. There are secret passages and hidden rooms! Let's explore together."

If you want to look for Homer, turn to page 35.

If you go with Anson, turn to page 67.

The bat spreads his wings and his eyes twinkle. You climb onto his back and fly through a window out of the house and high into the sky. You land in a garden. Big pieces of fruit cover the ground. The apples are red and yellow, and they're as big as cars. The pears are bigger than trucks!

You relax and take a huge bite out of a giant pear. You get soaked in pear juice. Ick! It's sticky. You lie out in the sun to dry off a bit, and then you decide to go exploring.

Turn to page 55.

You decide you don't really want to go off with the bat. Instead you hide in a dark room under a pile of old blankets and clothing. It's warm and comfortable. Soon you fall asleep.

When you wake up, you hear a noise. It sounds like thunder. The noise gets louder and louder. You see light under the door to the room. You open the door a crack.

Turn to page 59.

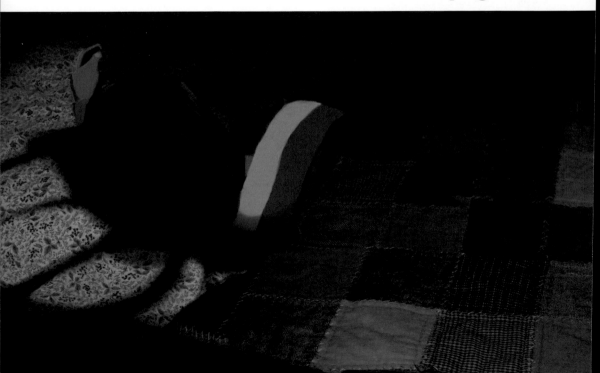

Good for you! You didn't know the turtle. You never know what could have been in those candies. The turtle eats the candy and turns into a rock.

You step over the rock and find a secret door in the wall. The door leads to the side yard of the house near the big trees. The sun shines on you. You are safe. You turn around and there is Homer! The mystery of Homer in the Haunted House is over.

The End

You certainly don't want to know what the furry thing is! You run up the stairs and go into a little room. Sun shines through a broken window. You see two kids. They smile at you, and one says, "Hi! Where did you come from?"

You tell them you came from downstairs.

"I don't want to go any farther. I'm scared," you say.

"Okay. Follow us." The two kids lead you to a secret staircase. It's dark and dusty. The climb up the stairs seems endless.

Turn to page 61.

You climb the sunbeam. The steps are made of gold, and they are just the right size for you.

The air is warm and smells good. You hear music playing. It sounds familiar, but you can't quite tell what the song is. It is so pleasant up on the sunbeam that you want to go on walking forever.

Turn to the next page.

Hold on! Shouldn't you turn back now? After all, what about Homer, and home, and school, and your friends?

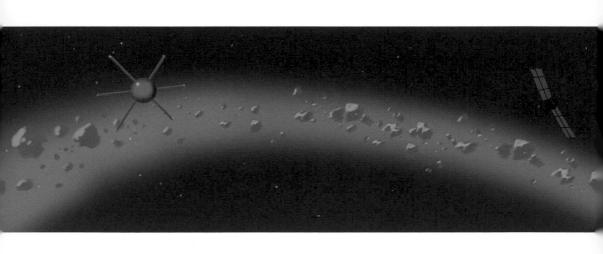

If you turn back, turn to page 63.

If you continue, turn to page 68.

"I'd love to go with you, but I have to find my dog," you tell Anson.

"I think I know where Homer is."

Anson leads you to a door on the second floor. There is a big sign that says:

ADMISSION
25 CENTS

Turn to the next page.

Anson pays for both of you. Wow! It's a movie about Superman. The place is jammed. Homer sits in the front row. There are two empty seats right next to him. Homer has saved them for you and Anson! He even brought you popcorn.

You settle back and enjoy the movie. What a great day you've had.

The End

You decide that it's safer on land than it is in the boat. At least you can walk wherever you want.

You walk down the bank of the river. It is muddy and gluppy. Two red eyes stare out at you from the water.

Snap!

Turn to the next page.

It's a crocodile. You jump back and hit the rocky wall of the tunnel. You are just far enough away from the crocodile to be safe.

Turn to page 9.

The mouse looks friendly, but you're not fooled. You are better off finding Homer on your own. The ladder is steep and hard to climb. As you climb, you hear the sound of wind above you. The wind rushes down the trapdoor, picks you up, and carries you upward.

Turn to the next page.

You spin in a white cloud. The cloud is soft, fluffy, and comfortable.

Soon the wind dies down, and it is quiet.
You float over the earth on your cloud bed.

Turn to the next page.

All of a sudden you are soaked. It is raining! The cloud gets smaller and smaller and you fall out. You ride the gentle rain back down to the haunted house.

What a trip! You hope you can remember everything that has happened. You can't wait to get home.

Homer runs up and licks your face. Ugh! Yucky dog lips!

The End

You get out of the boat and walk down the riverbank. You find a flower garden. Wow! Right in the middle of the garden is a funny-looking bus. It's more like a sausage on wheels. There's no driver, either. But you decide to get in.

Turn to the next page.

The bus takes you out of the garden and onto a big highway. In a snap of a finger you are whizzed to your own house. Homer is so excited to see you that he nearly knocks you over.

The End

You have a small flashlight in your pocket. Click! It's on. Wow! It's a furry turtle. The turtle has a goofy look on his face. He offers you a box of candy. "Go ahead. Eat one. It won't hurt you." (DANGER!! DANGER!!)

If you eat a piece of candy, turn to page 24.

If you don't eat the candy, turn to page 29.

You give the boat conductor 50 cents.

The boat has wings. You can actually fly it. You fly up to the sky and over the land. Right below you is your own house. Your mother is in the backyard. She waves at you. You land the boat in the yard.

"Welcome home," she says as she hugs you.

The boat leaves with a flutter of wings.

The End

There is a tunnel at one end of the room. A fat brown mouse appears in the opening of the tunnel. He says, "Follow me!"

If you follow the mouse down the tunnel, turn to page 18.

If you go back up the ladder, turn to page 39.

If you run by him and go down the tunnel alone, turn to page 70.

You're in luck! The red door opens into a circus. You see your whole family there. They are having a great time. You join a group of clowns. You are all in an act where you all squeeze into a mini-car. No one can believe when you fit your whole family and ten clowns into one small red car.

The End

The silver key is magic. When you hold it, you can fly to the top of the tallest mountain in the world. You can see for hundreds of miles! Finally you return to earth and your own home. Homer is in the front yard. He wags his tail, jumps up, and gives you a big, wet, sloppy kiss.

The End

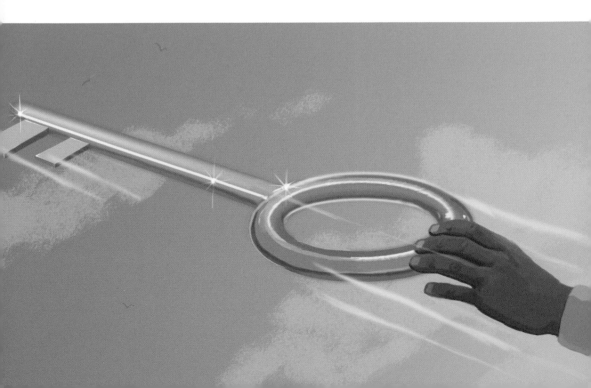

"Who are you?"

"Well, you see, I am the mayor of this town. I ask the same of you. Who, just who, are you to be eating our houses?"

You tell him your name.

He bows and shakes your hand.

"How do I get home from here?" you ask.

He says, "Just wish it, and you'll be there."

You close your eyes and wish and—*poof!*—you are home.

The End

Surprise! The yellow door opens onto the baseball field behind your school. You are in center field, and a ball is coming right at you.

You look up just in time and catch the baseball. Your team yells, "Hurray! We win!"

Turn to the next page.

Your teammates surround you and give you big hugs. You saved the game.

All the rest was a daydream you had while standing in center field. You can't wait to get home to see Homer!

The End

Amazing! You come upon a house made out of cream puffs. Next to the cream puff house is one made of éclairs. You take a taste of both houses. You stroll down the street. Everywhere you see houses made of your favorite desserts. What a great place!

Turn to page 57.

Then you hear a voice. It says, "Hey, don't eat my house, I live in it." When you look around, you see a small, strange man no bigger than a cat.

Turn to page 51.

Wake up! Fireworks. You look out your bedroom window. There are four kids setting off firecrackers.

Turn to the next page.

Of course! It's the Fourth of July.

You go back to sleep, wondering what you will dream next.

The End

Suddenly you come out on a porch.

There is a rope ladder on the railing. You drop the ladder to the ground and climb down.

Turn to the next page.

"Yip! Yip! Yip!" It's Homer. He is waiting for you outside. He is safe and so are you.

You wave goodbye to your friends. When you turn back, you see Homer chasing after another white cat.

Oh, no!

The End

The sunbeam turns into a giant slide.
WHOOOOOSH!

You end up in the fun house at the amusement park.

The End

You stick your finger into the crocodile's eye. "Yikes! That's not fair," he screams and lets go. You swim to shore and run along the bank. The crocodile climbs up the bank and follows you, crying. "I wasn't going to hurt you. I just wanted to play."

Go on to the next page.

A path on the riverbank leads outside. You are free. Homer is there. He licks your face. You won't go back to this old house. Not on your life!

The End

Anson leads you into a big room.

Surprise!! It's your birthday, and this is your party. All your friends gather around you. Your mom is holding the biggest chocolate cake you've ever seen. Homer is sitting at the head of the table. He looks ready to blow out the candles. Beat him to it!

The End

You decide to continue following the unicorn. At last it turns right and stops.

"There is the path to Venus. Follow it if you wish." Then it vanishes—*poof!*—in a puff of pink smoke.

You start to walk on the path. It is beautiful. Venus seems very small. Venus has windows and curtains and wallpaper and swimming trophies and—wait! It's your own room!

You sit up in bed. It was all a dream.

The End

Hurray for you! Good choice!

You chose the golden key and the door to safety. Homer runs up, wagging his tail. The tunnel has opened into your own backyard!

The End

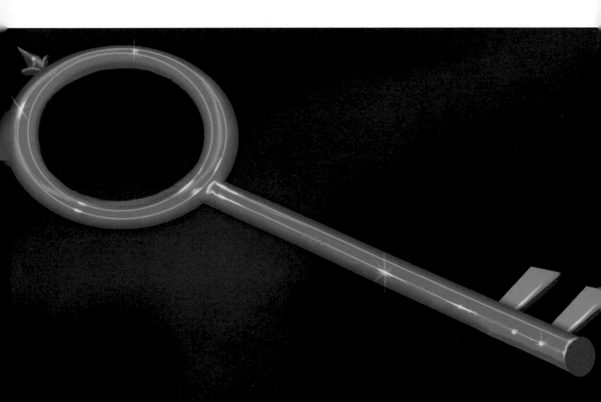

You leave the mouse and run down the tunnel alone. The tunnel leads into a room with two doors. One door is yellow and very big. The other is red and very small.

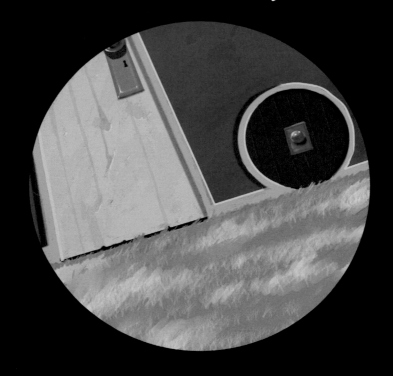

If you go through the red door, turn to page 49.

If you go through the yellow door, turn to page 52.

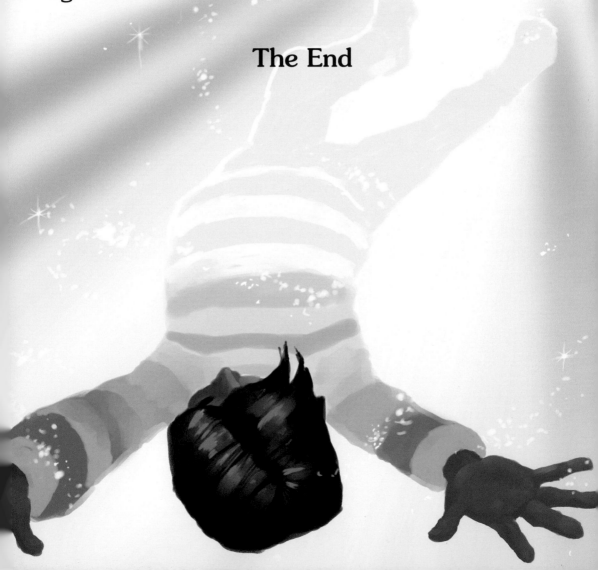

You can't turn back. You've climbed so far on the sunbeam that you become part of it. You sparkle and you shine, and you help light the world.

The End

ABOUT THE ARTIST

Keith Newton began his art career in the theater as a set painter.
Having talent and a strong desire to paint portraits, he moved to New
York and studied fine art at the Art Students League. Keith has won
numerous awards in art such as The Grumbacher Gold Medallion and
Salmagundi Award for Pastel. He soon began illustrating and was
hired by Disney Feature Animation where he worked on such films as
Pocahontas and *Mulan* as a background artist. Keith also designed color
models for sculptures at Disney Animal Kingdom and has animated
commercials for Euro Disney. Today, Keith Newton freelances from his
home and teaches entertainment illustration at The College for Creative
Studies in Detroit. He is married and has two daughters.

ABOUT THE AUTHOR

R. A. Montgomery attended Hopkins Grammar School, Williston-Northampton School and Williams College where he graduated in 1958. He pursued graduate studies in Religion and Economics at Yale and NYU. Montgomery was an adventurer all his life, climbing mountains in the Himalaya, skiing throughout Europe and scuba-diving wherever he could. His interests included education, macro-economics, geo-politics, mythology, history, mystery novels and music. He wrote his first interactive book, *Journey Under the Sea,* in 1976 and published it under the series name *The Adventures of You*. A few years later Bantam Books bought this book and gave Montgomery a contract for five more, to inaugurate their new children's publishing division. Bantam renamed the series *Choose Your Own Adventure* and a publishing phenomenon was born. The series has sold more than 260 million copies in over 40 languages. He was married to the writer Shannon Gilligan. Montgomery died in November 2014, only two months after his last book was published.

For games, activities, and other fun stuff, or to write to Chooseco, visit us online at CYOA.com

Watch for these titles coming up in the

CHOOSE YOUR OWN ADVENTURE®

Dragonlarks® series for Beginning Readers

"In a world where children have so little autonomy, my children found delight as they were given the choice to create their own adventure. . . . Fun! Fun! Fun!"

— cyoa.com

SEARCH FOR THE DRAGON QUEEN
DRAGON DAY
RETURN TO HAUNTED HOUSE
THE LAKE MONSTER MYSTERY
ALWAYS PICKED LAST
YOUR VERY OWN ROBOT
YOUR VERY OWN ROBOT GOES CUCKOO-BANANAS
THE HAUNTED HOUSE
SAND CASTLE
LOST DOG!
GHOST ISLAND
THE OWL TREE
YOUR PURRR-FECT BIRTHDAY
INDIAN TRAIL
CARAVAN
GUS VS. THE ROBOT KING
SPACE PUP
FIRE!
PRINCESS ISLAND

"My seven-year-ol son was captivated by the idea that he could have a hand in guiding a story about having his very own robot. Th story lines kept my son reading over an over. Well done!!!"

— cyoa.com

Purchase online at www.cyoa.com or ask your local bookseller